This 1995 edition published by Derrydale Books,
distributed by Random House Value Publishing, Inc.,
40 Engelhard Avenue, Avenel, New Jersey 07001
© 1994 Jane Wardle and Georgina Hargreaves.
Produced by Emma Books Ltd., Beckington, Somerset, U.K.
Illustrated by Georgina Hargreaves. Printed in Italy.
A CIP Catalog Record for this book is available from the Library of Congress.
ISBN 0-517-12063-1

Random House
New York • Toronto • London • Sydney • Auckland

Prince Brownie's Shoes

Written by Jane Wardle
Illustrated by Georgina Hargreaves

DERRYDALE BOOKS
NEW YORK • AVENEL

Prince Brownie was a very lively pony, always prancing, side stepping and generally playing around. Unfortunately, this usually meant that he wore his metal shoes out very quickly. The time had come for Prince Brownie to be shod again, but the blacksmith was not due at the farm for another week.

Jane decided to ask her mother if she could ride him over to the blacksmith to be shod early.

"I can take him after school if Mr. Cox can fit him in," Jane told her mother.

"Telephone first and make sure that you can see him early enough for you to get home before dark," her mother replied.

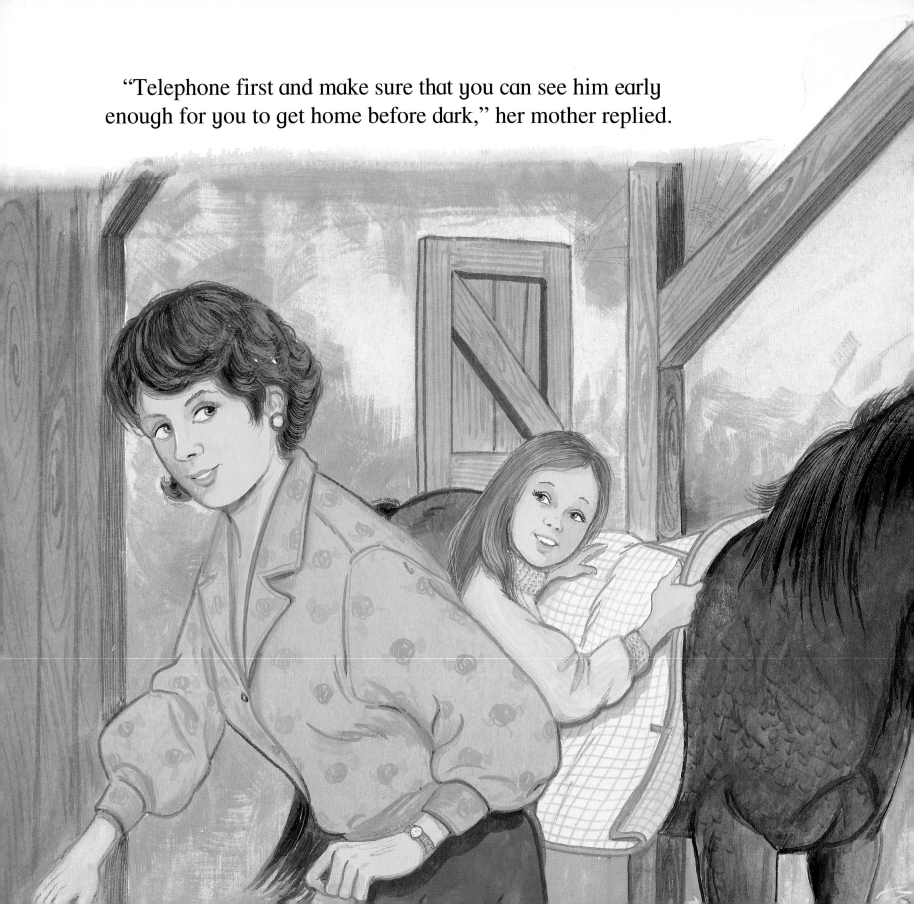

So the following afternoon, Jane and Prince Brownie set off for the blacksmith in the next town, over the open fields. It was a long ride out of town and because the pony's shoes were loose, they took their time. They arrived late, but the blacksmith did not mind and set to work immediately. The sound of metal banging on metal echoed throughout the smoke-filled shop.

Prince Brownie, who did not like being shod, was leaning all his weight against the blacksmith.

"Give it up, you cheeky old pony!" shouted the red faced man as he held the pony's front leg between his knees, "I won't get these shoes on if you play that silly game."

Jane held Prince Brownie's bridle and giggled as she kissed his velvet nose, "You just can't help yourself, can you?" she said

11

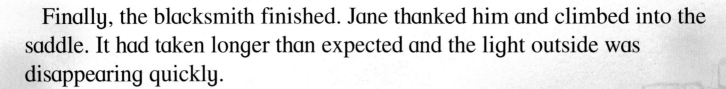

Finally, the blacksmith finished. Jane thanked him and climbed into the saddle. It had taken longer than expected and the light outside was disappearing quickly.

As the pair left through the gateway, two young boys who were riding past on their bicycles, skidded to a halt when they saw Prince Brownie and Jane, blocking their way.

"Let's get out of here!" shouted the larger of the two boys. Prince Brownie strode forward and towered above them, pawing the ground and flaring his nostrils.

The sight of Prince Brownie's solid chest, powerful legs and the glint in his eyes was enough for the boys.

Pedaling as fast as they could, knees pumping up and down like pistons, elbows sticking out at ninety degrees, they headed off in the other direction.

"You are the bravest pony in the world," Jane said as she patted his neck, "I feel that I can do anything when I am riding you."

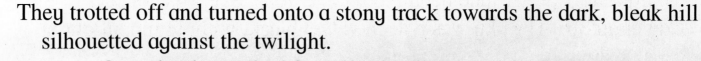

They trotted off and turned onto a stony track towards the dark, bleak hill silhouetted against the twilight.

Open land stretched for miles in all directions. Everywhere was quiet and still, the silence broken only by the sound of hooves on stones and Jane talking to her pony.

"I feel like a highway robber,' she said, and his ears flicked backward at the sound of her voice, "Just the two of us alone in the dark."

Each wall and bush seemed to hide dancing shadows. With the last of the light now gone, Jane began to feel nervous. She was not sure of the way anymore. The sky was a deep velvet black, without moonlight or stars to show them the way home.

Prince Brownie could feel Jane's knees gripping into the saddle and her fingers tightening on the reins, but his confidence did not waver. He needed no light at nighttime to guide him in his field and he did not need it to show him home now.

"Well, I think I will leave it up to you now," Jane told her pony as she gripped some of his thick black mane in her hands.

"Mom and Dad will not worry, they know that I will be all right riding you home."

But Jane began to have the creepy feeling that someone was following them. She did not want to hurry in case Prince Brownie slipped on the stony path. She turned her head nervously to see if she could see anything. There was nothing in sight, so, very cautiously, she began to relax.

Prince Brownie's swinging walk gave Jane some confidence. They turned to take a steep path that seemed to lead them to the top of the hillside.

At last they reached the top of the hill, and there below them were the golden and white lights of the town in the distance - at last Jane could see where they were going. Prince Brownie, sensing his warm stable and full hayrack waiting for him, broke into an eager trot. There were lights on at the stables as she approached and there waiting were her parents.

"Here they are," shouted her father. They trotted into the yard. The headlights from her parents' car lit up Jane's smiling face.

Everyone patted Prince Brownie and Jane leaned over to hug his neck. "He really is the smartest pony in the world," said Jane, "He was not at all frightened. It was almost as if he could see in the dark."